Layla's Head Scarf

By Miriam Cohen
Illustrated By Ronald Himler

STAR BRIGHT BOOKS
Cambridge Massachusetts

The name Star Bright Books and the Star Bright Books logo
are registered trademarks of Star Bright Books, Inc.
Please visit: www.starbrightbooks.com.
For bulk orders, please email: orders@starbrightbooks.com,
or call customer service at: (617) 354-1300.

Hardback ISBN-13: 978-1-59572-177-8

Paperback ISBN-13: 978-1-59572-178-5
Star Bright Books / MA / 00206160
Printed in China / WKT / 9 8 7 6 5 4 3 2

Printed on paper from sustainable forests.

Library of Congress Cataloging-in-Publication Data

Cohen, Miriam, 1926-
 Layla's head scarf / by Miriam Cohen ; illustrated by Ronald Himler.
     p. cm.
 Summary: New in first grade, shy Layla is reluctant to participate in class activities because she feels
her head scarf makes her look too different from her classmates.
 ISBN 978-1-59572-177-8 (hard back : alk. paper) -- ISBN 978-1-59572-178-5 (paper back : alk. paper)
[1. Clothing and dress--Fiction. 2. Self-confidence--Fiction. 3. Prejudices--Fiction.
4. Interpersonal relations--Fiction. 5. Schools--Fiction.] I. Himler, Ronald, ill. II. Title.
PZ7.C6628Lay 2009
[E]--dc22
                              2009004693

Dedicated to Laura Jackson, Shelia Kapur,
Jessie Staub, and Sandra Vizcaino at P. S. 27,
and Elizabeth O'Brien at P.S. 84.

— M.C.

First Grade sat in a circle.
They sang, "Where is Sara? Where is Sara?"
And Sara sang back, "Here I am! Here I am!
Very glad to see you, very glad to see you. Here I am!"

Jim was next. Then Anna Maria.
Everyone had a turn in the circle until it was Layla's turn.
"It's your turn, Layla!" they all said.
But Layla shook her head.

"She's shy because she's new," Jim whispered to Paul.
The teacher smiled at Layla and sang, "We're very
glad to see you, very glad to see you. Yes, we are!"

"It's library time!" said the teacher.
"Walk! Don't run!" she called.
 Everybody walked very quickly down the hall.

First Grade loved library time. They could pick any book
they wanted to read. Jim was interested in turtles.
"Look at this giant turtle! It's 50 years old."
"So what?" Danny said. "My uncle is 60 years old."
"But your uncle is not a turtle," said George.
 Everybody at the table laughed.

Danny asked, "Why don't you take your hat off, Layla?"
"It's not a hat. It's a scarf," Anna Maria said.
"She doesn't have to take it off if she doesn't want to."

Danny sat down next to Willy and Sammy. He showed them his book, *The World's Great Soccer Stars*.
"I'm a good soccer player," he boasted.
Willy and Sammy said, "We like baseball better. We're for the Mets. Who are you for?"
"Shhh," said the librarian.

Anna Maria was looking at *Puppies*.
"Aren't they cute? I love puppies."
"I love kittens," said Margaret.
George said, "My gramma has a kitten. She lives
in Chicago. Sometimes I go there for
vacation and . . ."
"Where is your book, George?" the librarian
asked.

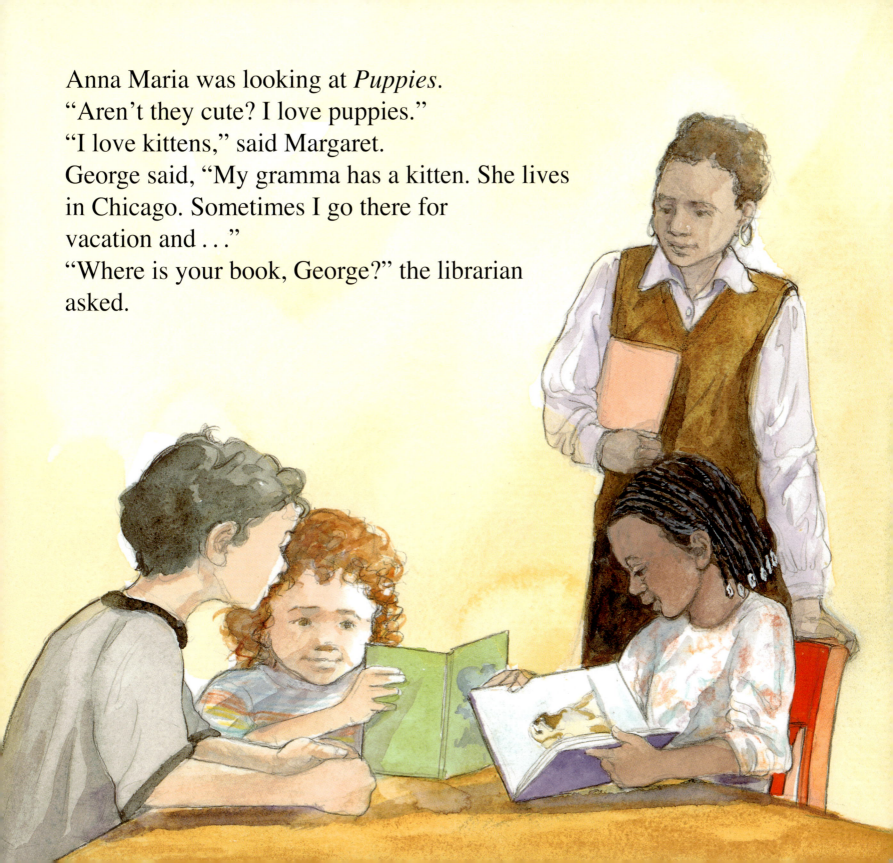

"Layla, here is a book you will like," said the librarian.
"It has pictures of the place where your family comes from."
Layla whispered, "Thank you."

The librarian held the book up for everyone to see.
It had pictures of a sandy, sunny land.
The trees were tall with tops like green feathers.
And there were lots of ladies with scarves.